TD **Bank Financial Group**

D1543714

Charlie Baillie
Chairman and Chief Executive Officer
TD Bank Financial Group

Dear Readers,

This book is just for you! It's a gift from TD to take home and treasure. I hope you enjoy books as much as I do. I especially hope you enjoy this book, *Young Authors' Day at Pokeweed Public School*. It's a story about students who love to read and celebrate their school's Book Week with a visit from their favourite author.

Everyone at TD is excited to give you and every grade one student in Canada this book. It's our way of celebrating TD Canadian Children's Book Week. We encourage you to visit your local library to discover the magical world of books and the fun of reading!

Have fun reading . . . just like the students at Pokeweed Public School!

Charlie Baillie

Charlie Baillie

Written by John Bianchi
Illustrated by John Bianchi
Copyright 1999 by Pokeweed Press

Cataloguing in Publication Data

Bianchi, John
    Young Authors' Day at Pokeweed Public School

(Pokeweed Public School)

ISBN 1-894323-32-7 (CCBW edition)
ISBN 1-894323-14-9 (bound)

    I. Title.   II. Series

PS8553.I26Y68 1999   jC813'.54   C99-901047-6
PZ7.B47126Yo 1999

Published by:
Pokeweed Press,
Suite 337
829 Norwest Road
Kingston, Ontario
K7P 2N3

Printed in Canada by:
Friesens Corporation

Visit Pokeweed Press on the Net at:
www.Pokeweed.com

Send E-mail to Pokeweed Press at:
publisher@pokeweed.com

Young Authors' Day at Pokeweed Public School

Written & Illustrated by

John Bianchi

Reading is so important at Pokeweed Public School that Ms. Mudwortz gives us some FRED each morning. FRED stands for Free Reading Every Day. When it's time for FRED, everyone finds a comfortable spot and settles down with a good book.

We all like different authors for different reasons.
Billy reads R.L. Mugs because his stories are so scary.

Buwocka always picks Tom Windysmith's books about sports.

Melody and I like the Mikki Merski Mysteries. We always try to see who can solve the mystery first.

But everyone loves Reginald Thornbottom's adventure books. Ms. Mudwortz says that his stories are so exciting, they are larger than life.

Each year, we devote a whole week to our school's young authors. The week ends with a visit by a real author. And this year — we could hardly believe it! — Reginald Thornbottom was coming to Pokeweed Public School.

We started the week with Writing Day.

Ms. Mudwortz said that before we began our stories, we needed an idea. An idea could be about anything — like a toy or a game or a bird — something that interested us.

Then we had to have three things.

I have a plant. I call my plant Nancy. Nancy likes water. Nancy hates bugs.

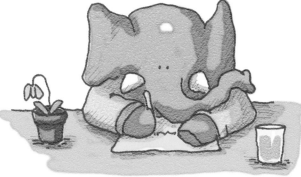

First, we needed a beginning. Ms. Mudwortz called this part the "introduction."

"Write something about your idea," she told us.

Next, we had to create a problem. Ms. Mudwortz explained that this would make the story a story.

2. One day, a bug landed on Nancy.

3.

I gave Nancy some water. The bug flew away.
The end

The last thing we had to have was a solution. "Great work!" said Ms. Mudwortz when she read Buwocka's story.

Tuesday was Picture Day, the day we "turned our words into pictures," as Ms. Mudwortz explained.

Then she gave us some tips:

"Make sure your character looks the same on each page."

"Try drawing your picture from very far away or very close up."

"Pretend you are a bird, looking down on your picture."

Wednesday was Book Day. We thought of a title for our story, we made a cover out of construction paper, and we bound our pages into real books.

On Thursday, FRED turned into RAT — Read Aloud Time. We each took turns reading our finished books to the class.

"A book is just a bunch of paper stuck together until someone reads it," said Ms. Mudwortz.

Then it was time to prepare for Reginald Thornbottom's visit. Since no one had ever seen a photograph of him, Ms. Mudwortz thought it would be fun for each of us to draw a picture of what we imagined he might look like. We couldn't wait to see who had come the closest.

Friday was Young Authors' Day.

Ms. Mudwortz assembled the band outside, and when we saw Reginald Thornbottom's car pull up, we all played *For He's a Jolly Good Fellow.*

"Welcome to Pokeweed Public School, Mr. Thornbottom," said Principal Slugmeyer, rushing him into the school.

"But . . . ," he replied.

"Time for a fast photo," ordered Principal Slugmeyer, as he arranged everyone in the library.

"But . . . ," said our guest, as the camera flashed.

Principal Slugmeyer hurried him to the auditorium and up onto the stage.

"Everyone's in place," said Principal Slugmeyer, looking out at the crowd.

"But . . . ," whispered our visitor.

As Ms. Mudwortz raised her hoof to silence everyone, Principal Slugmeyer made an enthusiastic introduction.

"Okay, everyone, let's put our paws and hooves together and give a warm Pokeweed Public School welcome to Mr. Reginald Thornbottom!"

"Thank you very much," our guest of honor began after an enormous ovation. "I'm pleased to be here. But I'm not Reginald Thornbottom!"

We all gasped.

"I'm Arthur, Mr. Thornbottom's driver."

"But . . . but what happened to Mr. Thornbottom?" asked Principal Slugmeyer. "Is he ill? Did he have an accident? Did he get lost?"

"Oh, no. He's right here," announced Arthur, opening the box he was carrying.

"Hello," squeaked Reginald Thornbottom as Arthur lifted him out.

"I . . . I thought that was a box of books," said Principal Slugmeyer, shaking the tiny author's paw.

"Of course not," corrected Mr. Thornbottom. "It's my office. Arthur takes me everywhere in it. The world is a dangerous place for a little book mouse like me. And besides, I never like to be far from my work — so I bring it with me!"

And with that, little Reginald Thornbottom
proceeded to give a great big presentation.
First, he showed us some pictures of where he lives
and where he does his work and some of the neat
places he has been.

Then he demonstrated some of his writing techniques.

He talked about how he always uses big sheets of paper so that he has lots of room to expand his ideas.

Finally, he read to us from his latest book. When his presentation was finished, we ended the afternoon with the annual Young Authors' Pizza Party.

Young Authors' Day was another classic Pokeweed Public
School success. Mr. Thornbottom even took the time to
read and autograph all our books.

I love what he put in mine. "Keep up the good work!" he
wrote. "And remember, you don't have to be big to write
stories that are larger than life."

TD Canadian Children's Book Week

TD Bank Financial Group and the Canadian Children's Book Centre (CCBC) are pleased to present this book in celebration of *TD Canadian Children's Book Week*, Canada's largest annual festival of reading and Canadian children's literature.

Each November, Canadian authors, illustrators and storytellers tour from coast to coast to meet tens of thousands of young readers and share the special joy of books created for and about Canadian children. For more information about Canada's largest literary event for children, including readings, book signings and other festivities in your area, visit the CCBC's Book Week web site at **www.bookweek.net**.

The Canadian Children's Book Centre is a national, non-profit organization founded in 1976 to encourage reading, inspire fine children's book writing and illustration, promote Canadian children's literature and help the Canadian children's book industry grow.

TD Canadian Children's Book Week is made possible through the generous support of the following sponsors and funders:

Title Sponsor: TD Bank Financial Group

Major Funder: The Canada Council for the Arts

Co-Associate Sponsors: Imperial Oil Charitable Foundation, Pearson Education Canada, The Toronto Public Library, the National Library of Canada, and the Ontario Arts Council.

Special thanks to Pokeweed Press for making this book available.

Visit: www.bookcentre.ca

Or write to: ccbc@bookcentre.ca.

About the writer and illustrator . . .

John Bianchi has been an avid artist from his earliest school days in Rochester, New York, where he entertained his classmates with caricatures of the teachers and students around him. In his twenties, he moved to Canada and became a full-time artist, selling his early work to tourists on the sidewalks of Ottawa. After a stint in an animation studio, he became a magazine illustrator.

He started illustrating and writing children's books in the mid-eighties and joined forces with editor Frank B. Edwards in 1986 to produce a long line of successful picture books that ranged from *The Bungalo Boys: Last of the Tree Ranchers* and *Princess Frownsalot* to *The Artist* and the *Pokeweed Public School* series. In 1999, he and Edwards launched Pokeweed Press as a vehicle to continue producing picture books that could be enjoyed by children and adults alike.

Together, John and Frank have produced 40 children's books. Both of them spend several weeks a year visiting schools to talk to students about their work.

For more information about John Bianchi and Pokeweed Press visit:

www.Pokeweed.com

The website includes special offers, activities for children, resource material and information on Pokeweed Press' line of children's picture books.